For Lyn, Chris and Angela,
From Your Little
Sister, Liz

First published in 2008 by Scholastic Children's Books
Euston House, 24 Eversholt Street
London NW1 1DB
a division of Scholastic Ltd
www.scholastic.co.uk

London ~ New York ~ Toronto ~ Sydney ~ Auckland
Mexico City ~ New Delhi ~ Hong Kong

My Little Sister, Doris

Liz Pichon

SCHOLASTIC

My big brother, Boris,
is being quite nice to me today.
We are playing **Croc Stars** in his room
when Mum and Dad come in.

"We have exciting news!" says Mum.

"Soon we will be hearing the pitter-patter
of tiny feet," says Dad.

"**Hooray**, we're getting a **pet!**" I cheer.
"**No, stupid!**" Boris snaps.
"We're getting a baby croc."
Then he points to the egg that Mum is holding.

Now that the egg has arrived,
I am suddenly not allowed to...

No running,
Little Croc!

run near the egg...

Too NOISY!

talk **loudly** near the egg...

play **guitar** near the egg..

...or do **any**thing that might disturb the egg.

Don't touch the egg, Little Croc!

"That egg is spoiling my fun," I tell Dad.

"Why don't you go and play with Boris?" he suggests.

But Boris has a "**new friend**" and doesn't want me around.

Busy...

Boris! Boris! Boris!

"**Agh!**"

So I go back to my room, but Mum has moved all my toys to make room for the baby croc.

"That's so not FAIR!" I cry.

I am **not** happy sharing with the egg. I'm supposed to be their Little Croc. Now I'll be Just Plain Moris.

With only half a bedroom.

"When the egg hatches, you'll have
so much fun together!" says Mum.

I don't think it'll be fun **at all**.

Mum suggests I sing my
favourite song to the egg.
"You have **such**
a wonderful voice," she says.
"I'm sure the egg will
love it too."

So while Mum is busy,
I start to sing.

Then suddenly the egg
begins to sway. I keep
singing and the egg
begins to roll,
and creak...

They all smile at my new baby sister, even Boris. But I am **not** smiling, because my snout is really hurting and nobody notices.

Every day, someone else comes
to fuss and coo over Doris.
   "She's adorable!" says Aunty Floris.
   "So cute!" adds Uncle Noris.
It's driving me mad because they
don't know what she's really like.

At night Doris wakes me up, crying and snuffling.

In the morning she plays with my toys.

She scribbles on my drawings...

...and snaps my pencils.

Stop that, Doris!

Doris throws my card collection in the air.

She pulls pages from my favourite books.

"Doris just wants to play with you," Mum tells me.

I wish she'd play with Boris instead.

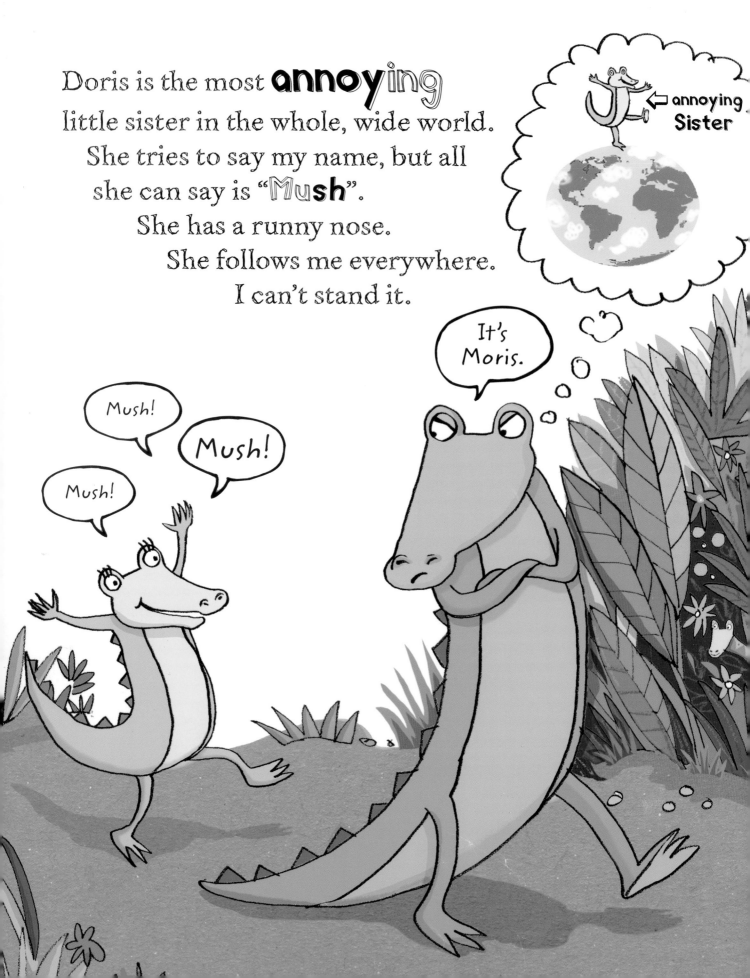

One day, she follows me into my room.
"No, Doris... not my guitar!"
But it's too late.
She snaps all the strings,
and I've had enough.

"AaGh!"

Snap!

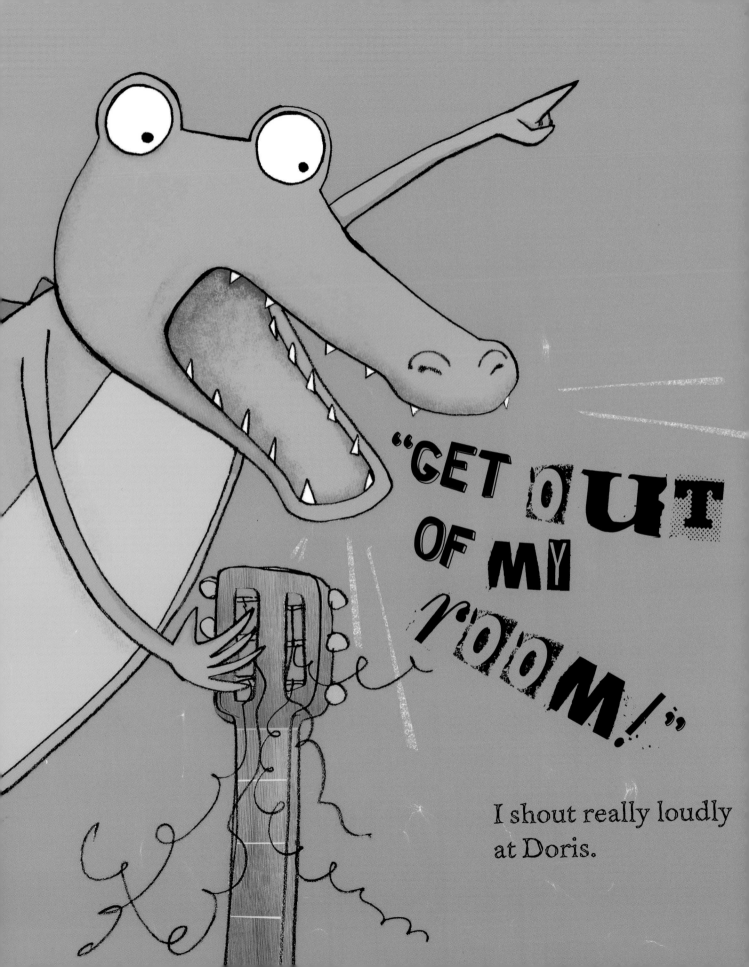

"GET OUT OF MY room!"

I shout really loudly at Doris.

She starts to cry.
Then Mum and
Dad tell **me** off for
upsetting my poor
little baby sister.
It's just **SO** unfair!

They make me stay in
my room to think
about what I've done.

"I wish Doris wasn't
my little sister"
is what I think.

...for the first
time ever, Doris says
my name properly...

After a long while,
Mum and Dad come
in to see me. Boris
has told them what
really happened.

They are sorry for
telling me off. Dad
helps me fix my guitar.

And then...

...and gives me a **big hug!**

So I show Doris how to play **Croc Stars**
And she is actually quite cool –
for a little sister.

Then Mum and Dad announce that
they have **one** more surprise
for me, in this really big box.

"We're all going to hear the pitter-patter of tiny feet again," they say excitedly.

"**Oh no**, not another egg!" I groan. I open the box very carefully…